SHIRE

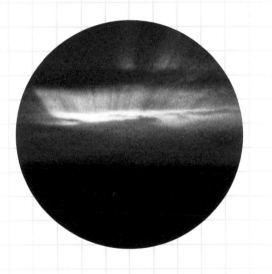

SHIRE

ALI SMITH

IMAGES BY
SARAH WOOD

FULL CIRCLE EDITIONS

For great poets do not die; they are continuing
presences; they need only the opportunity to walk
among us in the flesh.

Virginia Woolf

When the light is past
When the flower is shown
Let the poet be
Common earth and stone.

Olive Fraser

To keep in mind
Helena Shire
and Olive Fraser

for Isobel Murray

and for Sarah Wood

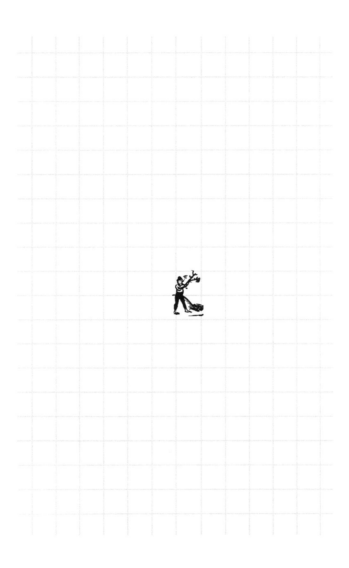

The beholder

I had been having difficulty breathing so I went
to the doctor. He couldn't find anything wrong.
My respiratory function tests came out clear
and strong. My heart was fine, my blood was
fine. My colour was fine.

Tell me again, about the breathing, he said.

It starts slight, then gets sorer and sorer,
I said. It's sore at the very top of my breath
then sore at the very bottom of my breath.
It feels like I've been winded. It's very
unpredictable. I never know when it'll come
or when it's going to go.

The doctor looked again at his computer
screen. He clicked his tongue.

And life generally? he asked. How's life?

Fine, I said.

Nothing out of the ordinary? he said.

No, I said, not really, well, my dad died and my siblings went mad and we've all stopped speaking to each other and my ex-partner is sueing me for half the value of everything I own and I got made redundant and about a month ago my next door neighbour bought a drum kit, but other than that, just, you know, the usual.

The doctor printed something out and signed it then handed it to me.

Take these, he said. Come back in a few weeks if life hasn't improved.

I went to Superdrug and they gave me a little box. In it was a blisterpack, three months' worth of antidepressant. I read the piece of paper that came with the blisterpack. It said that one of the side-effects was that these antidepressants would make you depressed. I left the pills unopened on the shelf in the bathroom.

The pain came and went. When it came I sat very still, if I could, and tried not to think of anything. But it's hard not to think of anything. I often ended up thinking of something.

I thought of us going through the old clothes in a wardrobe in his house and outside all the apples in the grass going soft, just falling off his trees because none of us had thought to pick them. I thought of the liquidiser on the sideboard in the kitchen back when we were married, a thing which we simply used, in the days when things were simple, to make soup. I thought of the sheen on the surfaces of the tables all pushed together in the meeting room and the way that when I came back to my desk nobody, not even the people I had thought were my friends, would look at me. I thought of sleep, how much I missed sleep. I thought how it was something I had never imagined about myself, that one day I would end up half in love with easeful sleep.

Yes, see that? the unexpected word easeful just slipping itself in like into a warm clean bed next to the word sleep. Easeful. It wasn't a straightforward word, the kind of word you hear much or hear people use often; it wasn't an easeful word. But when I turned it over on my tongue even something about its sound was easeful.

Then one day not long after I had surprised myself by crying about, of all things, how beautiful a word can be, I had just got up, run myself a bath and was about to step into it. I opened the top buttons of my pyjamas and that's when I first saw it in the mirror, down from the collarbone. It was woody, dark browny greeny, sort-of circular, ridged a bit like bark, about the size of a two pence piece.

I poked it. I stared at it in the mirror. I got the mirror down off the shelf and held it to my chest against myself.

I've no idea, the doctor said. I've never seen anything like it. It's definitely not a wart. I'm pretty sure it's not a tumour, at least it's nothing like any tumour I've seen.

He picked a pencil up off his desk. He sharpened the pencil. He poked me with the blunt end of the pencil and then the sharp end.

Ow, I said.

And it hasn't changed since you first noticed it? he said.

No, I said, apart from that it's got a bit bigger, and then these four little stubby branch things, well, they're new.

He left me in the room with the obligatory nurse and came back with two of the other doctors from the practice, the old one who's been there since the surgery opened and the newest youngest one, fresh from medical school. This new young doctor filmed my chest on her iPhone. The most senior doctor talked her through filing a little of the barky stuff into one sterilised tube then another. Then the most senior doctor and my own doctor each fingered the stubs until my doctor yelped. He held up his finger. At its tip was a perfect, round, very red drop of blood. While all three doctors ran round the room ripping open antiseptic packaging, the nurse, who'd been sitting against the wall by the screen, gently tested with the tip of her thumb the point of one of the thorny spikes on the stub furthest away from my chest.

Really remarkably sharp, she said quietly to me. Have they nicked you at all in the skin?

Once or twice, I said.

Does it hurt when they do that? she said.

Hardly, I said. Not on any real scale of hurt.

She nodded. I buttoned my shirt up again carefully over the stubs. That week I had ruined three shirts. I was running out of shirts.

The young and the old doctor left. The nurse winked at me and left. My own doctor sat down at his desk. He typed something into his computer with difficulty because of the size of the bandage on his finger.

I'm referring you to a consultant, he said. Actually – you might want to make a note – I'm going to refer you to several consultants at the following clinics: Oncology Ontology Dermatology Neurology Urology Etymology Impology Expology Infomology Mentholology Ornithology and Apology, did you get all that?

and when you see Dr Mathieson at Tautology, well, not to put too fine a point on it, he's the best in the country. He'll cut it straight out. You'll have no more problems. You should hear in the next ten days or so. Meanwhile, any discomfort, don't hesitate.

I thanked him, arranged my scarf over the bits of the stubs that were too visible through my shirt and left the surgery.

On my way to buy a new shirt, I met a gypsy. She was selling lucky white heather. She held out a sprig to me.

I'm sorry, I've no money, I said.

Well, she said looking me up and down, you've not got much, true enough, I can see that. But you've a kind face, so money's the least of your worries. Give me everything you've got in your pockets and that'll be more than enough for me.

I had two ten pound notes in my purse and a little loose change in one of my pockets. I gave her the change.

Ah but what about those notes? she said.
I can see them in your wallet, you know.

Can you? I said.

Burning a hole in you, she said.

If I give you all my money I'll be broke, I said.

Yes, you will, she said.

She held out the heather. I took it. It was
wrapped at the stem in a little crush of tinfoil
warm from her hand. She took my money and
she tucked it into her clothes. Then she stood in
front of me with her hands up in benison and
she said:

May the road rise to meet you, may the
wind always be at your back, may the sun shine
warm upon your face, may the rains fall
soft upon your fields, and until we meet again
may absence make your heart grow, and I think
that may well be a very nice specimen you've
got there in your chest, if I'm not wrong,
a young licitness.

A young what? I said but a couple of
community police oficers were strolling up the

street towards us and she was busy tucking away her sprigs of heather into her many coat pockets, in fact it looked like her coat was more pocket than coat.

Give it a few hours of sun every day if you can, she called back over her shoulder as she went, stay well hydrated and just occasionally you'll need to add some good well-rotted manure and cut yourself back hard, but always cut on the slant, my lovely. All the best, now.

What did you say it was, again? I called.

But she was well gone; it wasn't until a bit later when I chanced to be whiling away an early spring afternoon wandering around in the park that I saw what I was looking for and found the right words for it. Meanwhile the letters from the clinics arrived, the first, then another, then another, then another, and as they came through the letterbox I piled them unopened on the hall table. Meanwhile the pairs of little stubby antlers grew and greened and notched themselves then split and grew again, long and slender, as high as my eyes, so that putting on a jumper took ten very careful minutes and I began to do a lot of improvisation with cardigans and V-neck vest-tops. There were elegant single buds at the ends of thin lone stems closed tight on themselves, and a large number of clustered tight-shut buds on some of the stronger thicker branches. My phone went off in my pocket and as I reached in, took it out, pressed Answer, arched my arm past the worst of the thorns and got the phone to my ear pretty much unscratched, the whole rich tangled mass of me swung and shifted and shivered every serrated edge of its hundreds and hundreds of perfect green new leaves.

Hello, a cheery voice said. I'm just doing a follow-up call after your visit and your tests earlier this month, so if you could just let us know whether there've been any changes or developments in your condition.

Yes, I said, a very important development, I know what it is now, it's called a Young Lycidas, it's a David Austin variety, very hardy, good repeater, strong in fragrance, quite a recent breed, I was in Regent's Park a couple of days ago and I saw it there, exactly the same specimen, I wrote down what the label said and when I got home I looked it up, apparently they named it only a couple of years ago after the hero of Milton's elegy about the shepherd who's a tremendous musician but who gets drowned at sea at a tragically young age.

Em –, the voice said.

Then there was a pause.

The other thing about Milton, I said, is that he was a great maker-up of words, and one of the reasons they named a rose after him, not just because it was an anniversary of his birth or death, I can't remember which, in 2008, is that he's actually the person who invented, just made up, out of nothing, the word fragrance. Well, not out of nothing, from a Latin root, but you know what I mean.

I waited but nobody spoke, so I went on.

And gloom, I said. And lovelorn, and even the

word padlock we wouldn't have, if it wasn't for him just making it up. I wonder what we'd call padlocks if we didn't call them padlocks.

Then the voice began saying something serious-sounding about something. But I wasn't listening, I had seen a bird above the green of me, a swift, I saw it soar high in the air with its wings arched and I remembered as if I were actually seeing it happen again in front of my eyes something from back when we were first married, on holiday in Greece having breakfast one morning in our hotel.

It's a warm windy morning, it must be very windy because the force of the wind has grounded a swift, the kind of bird that's never supposed to land, a young one, still small. In a moment you're up on your feet, you drop your knife against your plate, cross the courtyard and scoop the bird up in both hands; it struggles back against you and a couple of times nearly wings itself free, but you cup it gently back in again, its head surprisingly grey and its eyes like black beads in the cup of your hands; I have never seen and am unlikely ever again to see a swift so clearly or so close. You carry it up the several flights of stairs till we get to the open-air roof of the building, you go to the very edge of the roof with it and then I see you throw your arms up and fling the bird into the air.

For a moment it rose, it opened its wings and held the wind. But then it fell, it was too young, the wind was still too strong for it. We ran down all those stairs as fast as we could and went out into the street to look for it, we looked all up and down the street directly below, but we couldn't find it. So god knows whether it made it. God knows whether it didn't.

Hello? the voice was saying more and more insistent, more and more officious in my ear, hello? but I was looking open-mouthed at the first burst of colour, a coiled whorl of deep pink inches away from my eyes, rich and layered petal after petal in the unfold of petal.

The scent was, yes, of roses, and look,

four new buds round this opened flower had appeared too, I'd not noticed them till now and they looked as if they were really ready to open, about to any minute.

Yes, I said into the phone. Sorry. Hello.

Urgency, update, condition? the voice said.

Fine, I said. Life's fine. Life has definitely improved.

Yes, but. Results, hospital, inconclusive, the voice said. Urgent, immediate, straightaway.

The voice had become implacable.

Surgery policy, the voice said.

Then it softened.

Here, it said. Help.

Well, I said, for now I'm okay though at some point soon I might need a bit of a hand with some trellissing.

With – ? the voice said.

I'm so sorry, I said, but I'm on a train and we may lose reception any mo –

I pressed the End Call button then switched my phone off because all four of those new buds had opened right before my eyes and I was annoyed that because I had been talking on a phone I had not seen a single one of them do it.

I have never yet managed to see the moment of the petals of a bud unfurling. I might dedicate the rest of my life to it and might still never see it. No, not might, will: I will dedicate the rest of my life, in which I walk forward into this blossoming. When there's no blossom I will dead-head and wait. It'll be back. That's the nature of things.

As it is, I am careful when kissing, or when taking anyone in my arms. I warn them about the thorns. I treat myself with care. I guard against pests and frost-damage. I am careful with my roots. I know they need depth and darkness, and any shit that comes my way I know exactly what to do with. I'm composed when it comes to compost.

Here's my father, a week before he died. He's in the hospital bed, hardly conscious. Don't wake me, he says, whatever you do.

He turns over away from us, his back to us. Then he reaches down into the bed as if he's adjusting one of the tubes that go in and out of him and, as if there's nobody here but him – can he really be – the only word for it isn't an easeful word, it's the word wanking. Whatever he's doing under the covers for those few seconds he takes, it makes the word wank beautiful. He's dying. Death can wait.

A branch breaks into flower at the right hand side of my forehead with a vigour that makes me proud.

Here we all are, small, on the back seat, our father driving, we're on holiday. There's a cassette playing: The Spinners; they're a folk band from tv, they do songs from all over the world. They do a song about a mongoose and a song about the aeroplane that crashed with the Manchester United team on board the time a lot of them died. That's a modern ballad, our father has told us, and there's a more traditional ballad on that same cassette too, about two lovers who

die young and tragically and are buried next to
each other in the same graveyard, that's the song
playing right now in the car in the July dark as we
drive back to the caravan site, the man from The
Spinners singing the words *and from her heart
grew a red red rose. And from his heart grew a briar.
They grew and they grew on the old church wall.
Till they could grow no higher.* When we get back
to the caravan and get into our beds in the smell
of toothpaste and soap-bags, when the breathing
of all the others regulates and becomes rhythmic,
I will be wide awake thinking about the dead
lovers, they are wearing football strips, bright red,
and their hearts are a tangle of briars and thorns,
and one of my brothers shifts in his sleep and
turns to me in the makeshift bed and says from
somewhere near sleep, are you having a bad
dream? and then though I don't say anything at
all he takes me and turns me round, puts one
arm under me so my head is on his shoulder and
his other arm across my front, and that's how he
holds me, sleeping himself, until I fall asleep too.

Every flower open on me nods its heavy head.

I lie in my bed in a home I'm learning to let go of and I listen to my neighbour playing the drums through the wall in the middle of the night. He's not bad. He's getting better, getting the hang of it.

Every rose opens into a layering of itself, a dense-packed grandeur that holds until it spills. On days that are still I can trace, if I want, exactly where I've been just by doubling back on myself and following the trail I've left.

But I prefer the windy days, the days that strip me back, blasted, tossed, who knows where, imagine them, purple-red, silver-pink, natural confetti, thin, fragile, easily crushed and blackened, fading already wherever the air's taken them across the city, the car parks, the streets, the ragged grass verges, dog-ear and adrift on the surfaces of the puddles, flat to the gutter stones, mixing with the litter, their shards of colour circling in the leaf-grimy corners of yards.

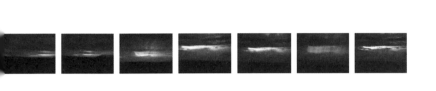

The poet

So she'd taken the book and she'd thrown it
across the room and when it hit the wall then
fell to the floor with its pages open it nearly
broke, which was one of the worst things you
could do, maybe a worse thing even than
saying a blasphemous curse, no, than saying
a blasphemous curse in a church, or near a
church, to break a book.

And she was a strong lass and she had a good
throw on her, as good a throw as a boy any day,
easily as good as thon holiday boy she'd shoved
into the river. For he might be at school down
south but that didn't mean no folk knew Latin
north of Edinburgh, did it, they had the Latin up
here as well, not that he even knew what he
claimed to anyway. *Aut insanit homo, aut versus
facit* she'd said and he'd looked at her blank-like,

the so-called boy scholar who'd never heard of
Horace, who said *pater* and *mater* to rhyme with
alli*gator*, with the *mater* and the *pater vacationing*
in *Nairn*shire, so *taken* with the *area*, and then
he'd said the thing about highland girls and
looked at her to let her know he'd a liking, the
cheek of it. For he might have a father a famous
surgeon but that meant nothing when you'd no
need of a surgeon, aye, and no need of a father
either, or a mother. And were all Edinburgh boys
that feart to hang off the parapet of a bridge by
their arms? He was too feart even to try, him and
his sister afraid to climb even a tree, and a girl
afraid of a tree was one thing, but a boy? *Oh no,*
his clothes he said and his sister with her painted
face and her talk of *boyfriends,* standing doing a
dance, *everybody's doing it back at home, don't you*
know it, Olive, really truly don't you up here och
dear me that's too too, then she started doing it,
a mad thing with her shoulders and her legs,
right there in the long grass at the river, the
midges jazzing up and down in a cloud above

the sister's head, and then the brother joined in, he knew the steps and all, he shimmied up the river bank away from the sister, took her own arm as if to make her do it with him and then – well, then he'd found himself in the river, him and his good clothes too.

Then she'd run for home, blasphem-o blasphem-as blasphem-at, over and over under her breath to the sound of her own feet hitting the path past the ruined church, blasphem-amus, blasphem-atus, blasphem-ant, it wasn't grammatical or real Latin like but it made a fine sound. She was laughing some, though she was shocked a bit at herself for doing it, in her head she could see the shock on the face of the boy from the cold of the water when he scrambled to his feet on the slippy stones, the water had darkened his good trews and his jacket too all up the side of himself he'd fallen on.

But when she was blasphemating up the High Street she saw the father of the man who was her father. He had his back to her, he was looking in the windows of the butcher's. And when she got back to the house her Aunt was out and her mother she could hear shifting about upstairs like a piece of misery as usual, and something, a badness, had come over her right then and she'd hated them all (except her Aunt, she'd never hate her Aunt) and she'd gone to the shelf where the books were kept and she'd taken the first one off the shelf her hand had come to and she'd thrown it.

And the book had broken right open and that's when she'd seen there was a music inside it, one nobody knew about, one you could never have guessed at, that was part of the way that the book had been made.

They were Fraser books. They'd sent them, the Frasers. There were books, and good new clothes too came to the house sometimes, and one day last month – it wasn't a birthday, it was well past her birthday, but Aunt said it would be meant for her sixteenth – there was even a watch, Aunt said a real gold one and put it away upstairs in its velvet in its hard box still in the shop wrapping from Aberdeen, for they knew otherwise it'd end in the river or buried in sand on the beach, sand choking its dainty face and nobody finding it for who knows how many summers or winters, if ever.

St Agnes Eve! Ah, bitter chill it was. The owl, for all his feathers, was a-cold. The hare limp'd trembling through the frozen grass. That was the poem Keats had written, about her birthdate, 20 January, four long months ago now her birthday, and one thing certain, time meant a lot more than the face of a wee gold watch, aye they could send a watch fine, even one that'd obviously cost a fair bit, but if they saw her in the street they'd look right through her, her father too. Since she was a quite wee girl he'd been back and as close as Flemington right up the road, so close a bird would hardly notice it, hardly have to use its wings if it crossed the sky from here to there.

But he may as well still be in Australia with

the sheep for all the difference his coming back made to his daughter, in fact she wished he were, so there'd be no danger of seeing him, no chance of him and his not-seeing of her in any street so close to home. She wished him thousands of miles away from here, truthfully she wished him on Algol, the bad most evil star in the sky, and her mother too, they could go and live there just the two of them happily never after, happily never exchanging a single word with each other for as long as they lived and nobody else would have to care. They could just go, the both, and take all their unsaying with them. For if a flower grew near them, even just the air that came from them would wither that flower.

But did that mean she would wither things too? Did a badness pass from them to her?

Would it ruin the feel of the mouth of the hill pony on the palm of her hand when she went the hike by herself and gave it the apple she had for her lunch, the bluntness of the mouth, the breath of it, the whiskers round the mouth she could feel, the warm wet and the slaver on her hand that she wiped on her skirt and got into the trouble about?

And the nest shaped like a dome, something that the bird just made without needing to know, without reading in a book how to make, and made it so solid and hung it so firm in the thinnest of the branches over the river?

There was the word gorgeous, and there was the word north, and there was a sound that went between the words that she liked: could you wither a word?

There was the orchard nobody went to. What could ruin an orchard like that one? It was all blossom right now. There was the whole meadow full of flowers, wild ones, all their bright faces beyond this house only a couple of streets away. She sat low on the old nursing chair and the Fraser books sat on the shelf right next to her eye. Fraser. Olive. O LIVE. I LOVE. O VILE. EVIL O.

She reached and took out the first book. She didn't even look at it, she threw the book. She just threw it.

And that's how, when the spine fell off it and she picked it up to look at the bad damage she'd done, she saw – the music, there.

Inside, behind the spine, the place where the pages were bound was lined with it, notes and staves all the way down the place the name of the book had been covering. There'd been a music inside it all the years the book had been in the world. And that was a fair few years, for on one of its first pages was the date 1871. So that made it fifty four years, near sixty, there'd been music nobody'd known about in the back of – she looked at the broken piece of spine – Walter Scott's Ivanhoe it was. And the paper with the notes and staves on it looked like it might be a good bit older than the book whose spine it was hidden in, for there was a quality to the way the notes were formed that didn't look like these things looked nowadays.

That was an e, but she didn't have the beginning of the stave so she didn't know what key. C#, f, e, c#, b, b, f#, a. Then the piece of music ended where the paper had been cut to fit the spine. On the surviving bit of stave below: a, a, e, g, b, e, b.

The clean closed spines of all the Scotts, book after book quiet and waiting, lined three shelves. She shouldn't even be in the front room. It was kept for the good. It wasn't used. She went to the space on the shelf that Ivanhoe had left. She put her finger to the top of the spine of the book next to the space. She tipped the book out, watched it balance on its own weight then fall. She caught it in her hand. Waverley Novels. The Heart of Mid-Lothian. She ran her hand over the good spine. The paper of it felt like brushed leather. It looked expensive. It looked like it would never break.

You could not tell whether there was music inside it just by looking at it.

(The boy's face, surprised by the cold of the

water. The dipper's nest overhanging the river, disguised by leaves in summer, bare to the eye in winter. The carcasses hanging in the butcher's window with the red and the white where the meat met the fat. The workings of the watch in its box in the dark.)

She looked at how well the stitching of the binding met the spine on the book in her hand. She gave it a tug with her fingers.

She went to the kitchen to get the gutting knife.

*

Olive Fraser, born twentieth of January 1909, Aberdeen. Died ninth of December 1977, Aberdeen.

Brought up by her beloved aunt, Ann Maria Jeans, in Redburn, Queen Street, Nairn, on the Moray Firth coast in the Scottish highlands. Estranged parents leave her there when they emigrate (separately) to Australia, and continue to do so after they come back (still estranged).

A headlong kind of a girl, a force of energy

and adventure. *That lassie lives in figures of speech.* Blue-eyed blonde, so eye-catching that the newly instated Rector of the University of Aberdeen (which is where she goes in 1927 when she's finished school, to study English), who happens to be driving past in his carriage from his own Instatement Ceremony, turns his head and cranes his neck to catch another glimpse of the startlingly beautiful girl in the crowd.

A talker. A livewire. *She was a beauty, but she gave the men a run for it.* Hilariously funny. A poet. Circle of admiring undergraduates at her feet and her lines spilling out of her all Spenserian stanza. Annoying to young men in seminars: *she niver thocht that up hersel, far did she get it fae?* Beloved of landladies (and simultaneously disapproved of): *that Miss Fraser! she keepit awfa 'ours.* Bright, glowing like a lightbulb, ideas flickering like power surges. When trying to string fishing line on a rod and reel in her student lodgings, tangles herself up so badly that she has to toss a coin out of a window

to a passing boy to get him to send a telegram
to her friend Helena who's a couple of years
younger and a writer herself and enthralled by
her exciting older poet friend: *imprisoned in digs.*
Please rescue. Olive. Recalls, much later in life,
this younger friend's happy family house in
Aberdeen, the welcoming shouts and the
laughter, the merriness, the warmth. Recalls the
singing of her friend's mother and the lucky
stone with a hole in it that her friend's mother
gives her before her final exams.

Outstanding student. 1933: to Girton
College in Cambridge on scholarship money,
though a couple of years remain unaccounted
for in between Aberdeen and Cambridge – poor
health? poverty? mental exhaustion?
Intermittently ill. Pale. Fatigued for no reason.
Five days of psychoanalysis in London: *he*
simply took my mind to pieces and built it up again.
I really feel as if I had been presented with a new
heaven and a new earth, ten thousand cold showers
on spring mornings and a Tinglow friction brush

(mental). Gains reputation as talented young poet. Wins University of Cambridge Chancellor's Medal for English Verse in 1935, only the second female student ever. Poem is called The Vikings. Senate unused to presenting anything to women : *a kind of quasi academic dress had to be devised*. Takes to calling herself Olave. Makes many new friends. Gets on many new people's nerves: *she was a pain in the neck.* Strongly dislikes Cambridgeshire: too flat, too dank, too inland. Strongly dislikes Girton (remembers it ten years later, in a poem called On a Distant Prospect of Girton College, like this: Here does heavenly Plato snore, / A cypher, no more. / … / Here sits Dante in the dim / With Freud watching him. / … / Here does blessed Mozart seem / Alas, a sensual dream.) Girton, in turn, strongly dislikes her: *she wasted the time of promising young scholars.*

Bad headaches. Grey skin. Nosebleeds. Concentration lapses. Unexplained illness. Fatigue.

Drifts from job to job. Back north to help on farm. Trains polo-ponies in Oxfordshire. Assistant to archaeologist in Bedford. Wartime: applies to cypher dept in Royal Navy WRNS in Greenwich. Posted to Liverpool, junior officer on watch, a witness to the blitzing of the maternity hospital near Liverpool docks. *Went out of her mind … thought the enemy were after her, trying to get in touch with her.* 1945: Poultry worker. 1946: Bodleian librarian (gets the sack, leaves under a cloud). Solderer. Assistant Nurse. Cleric. Shop girl (Fortnum's, among others). 1949: living in Stockwell Street, Greenwich (now demolished) then Royal Hill, Greenwich. *Made most of the furniture myself, being employed by a firm that had its own sawmill and was very generous in a thoughtful kind way to its employees and even to people who lived around.* The death of the mother. The death of her aunt. The death of her dog, Quip, an Irish Terrier. Drawn to Roman Catholicism; poetry becomes devotional. Poverty. *One new outfit in the last twelve years.*

1956 in London: onset of severe mental illness. *I was walking along and I just blacked out and when I came to, I found myself up a tree.* Diagnosed with schizophrenia. Hospitalized. *I cannot write any literature. It is as though I had lost a limb.* Medication: chlorpromazine. Like being *hammered down in a box and dropped below the Bermuda Deep.* Unrecognisable, *changed from the gallant, yellow-haired, rosy-cheeked girl. Grossly overweight, disfigured.* Medication brings on painful sensitivity to sunlight. Puffy eyes. Skin grey, leathery. Stuffs enough hospital teddy bears (paltry sum per bear) nearly to ruin her hands. Buys herself ticket north.

1960s: moves from house to uneasy house, renting in Inverness, Capital of the Highlands, sixteen miles from Nairn. Hospitalized again. Seen in grounds of Craig Dunain, Inverness mental hospital, wandering about holding beaten-up typewriter. Moves back to Aberdeen, this time to Cornhill hospital. *Percipient woman doctor*

thinks schizophrenia might be misdiagnosis and
medicates for hypothyroidism, myxoedema. *As if
by disenchantment* herself again.

Sunlight. *Three wonderful years of good health.*

Cancer. Two operations. Dies in December
1977. Penniless at time of death. Friends gather
in snow for funeral that never takes place: bad
weather, mishap, misinformation, accident.

Winner, over the years, of twenty two literary
prizes and two gold medals. Very little work
published. *When I send a poem to a publisher with
"Royal Mental Hospital" at the top …*

I have forgotten how to be / A bird upon a
dawn-lit tree, / A happy bird that has no care /
Beyond the leaf, the golden air. / I have forgotten
moon and sun, / And songs concluded and
undone, / And hope and ruth and all things save
/ The broken wit, the waiting grave.

*

In her medal-winning poem, The Vikings, the dead
are simultaneously ancient and young, *younger*

than death and life. The poem's narrator asks them
how it's possible that they're so very beautiful:

> O we are loved among the living still,
> We are forgiven among the dead. We
> > plough
> In the old narrows of the spirit. We
> Have woven our wealth into your mystery.

Here are three of her poems, the first from 1943,
the second circa 1954, the third 1971.

The Pilgrim

> I have no heart to give thee, for I
> Am only groundmists and a thing of
> > wind,
> And the stone echoes under bridges and
> > the kind

> Lights of high farms, the weary
> > watchdog's cry.

I have no desire for thy dreams, for my own
Are no dreams, but realities which are
The blind man's sight, the sick man's
                          heavenly star
Fire of the homeless, to no other known.

The poet (III)

Go to bed, my soul,
When the light is done.
Sleep from enemies
Blanketed in bone.

Let thy blood grow cold
As a mouldering stone
On a martyr's tomb,
Known to God alone.

On the stair of truth
Down and up are one.
Bless the cobbled street
When the light is gone.

When the light is past
When the flower is shown
Let the poet be
Common earth and stone.

The Unwanted Child

I was the wrong music
The wrong guest for you
When I came through the tundras
And thro' the dew.

Summon'd, tho' unwanted,
Hated, tho' true
I came by golden mountains
To dwell with you.

I took strange Algol with me
And Betelgeuse, but you
Wanted a purse of gold
And interest to accrue.

You could have had them all,
The dust, the glories too,
But I was the wrong music
And why I never knew.

*

The story about her finding the music in the
spines of the books is made up by me.

But that 1871 edition of Scott, like many
books over the centuries bound with recycled
old paper stock, really is lined and pasted with
staved manuscript at the back of the pages,
at least the couple of volumes I've got on my
desk both are.

And she really could, as a girl, hang from the
parapet of a Nairn bridge by her arms, and
pretty much everything else here can be found
and is sourced in the collections of her poems
which her good friend from her university years
in Aberdeen and Cambridge, the medieval and
renaissance academic Helena Mennie Shire,
edited after Olive Fraser's death, *The Pure*

Account (1981) and *The Wrong Music* (1989).

Think of the Waverley collection on the shelves, the full twenty five novels, their spines sliced back and open and the music inside them visible.

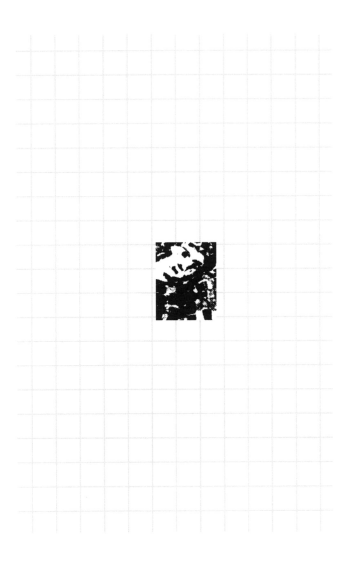

The commission

This was back when I was still a Catholic;
I know because it began one light spring evening,
I think probably in 1988, when I came out of the
front door of the church on Hills Road, St Mary
and the English Martyrs, ahead of everyone else
straight after Communion without waiting for
the final prayers (a ropey kind of Catholic) to
meet you where you usually waited for me on the
brick wall by the traffic junction.

You were talking to a spry-looking elderly
lady who turned and watched me come down
the steps of the church. The elderly lady was
blonde-grey and bright at the eye. She noticed
my accent. She asked me where I was from.
You introduced me to her and told her we'd met
when I'd written a play and you'd directed it,
and about how we were planning to take that

play to the Edinburgh Fringe later this year.
When she spoke again I could hear in her voice
that she was Scottish too, probably east coast.

Her name was Helena Shire; she'd taught
you Medieval Literature last year, when
you were in your first year, and she was a
Fellow at Robinson, the college you were at.
She invited us both to come to lunch there
a couple of weeks later.

One of the things about Mrs Shire was that
she always looked prepared, you say:

> I think of seeing her walking home across a
> field next to the College, her coat buttoned
> up against autumn and her bag dapperly
> slung across her like a satchel or like a
> person would wear setting out on a
> walking holiday in another time.

We went for lunch one Sunday soon after.
We ate in the refectory in Robinson, surely the
coolest college in Cambridge, not just because

you went there but also because of its John Piper stained glass in the chapel and the way the college had been built with money donated not by kings or aristocrats but by a Cambridge man who'd made an unexpected fortune selling and repairing bicycles.

The lady was charming, interesting, very witty, very funny. She told me she had studied, like I had, at Aberdeen as an undergraduate, that she'd been brought up in Aberdeen and had come down here to Cambridge to study at Newnham (which was the college I was now at) fifty-five years ago. She paid for our lunch then she took us upstairs to her bright college rooms and gave us coffee. I remember there were books about the Marx Brothers on her coffee table. One of them was a book of stills from their earliest films. I had this same book at home. I had never met anybody else who had this same old American book as I had, or anyone else who might actually want to read about or know about the Marx Brothers.

When we were leaving, the lady I'd now met a total of twice and known for about two hours handed me a sealed envelope.

Don't open it till you get home, she said.

I did as I she told me and opened it when I got back to our student house. Inside there was a cheque for a substantial amount, three hundred pounds I think, though I can't remember for sure. I remember it was easily enough to live on, food wise, for three or four months.

I phoned the lady from the big grey coinbox phone installed in our hall cupboard, which was our landlord's way of avoiding being left with bills in a student house whose turnover of tenants was high.

It's far too kind. I can't possibly accept this, I said.

Yes you can, she said. Don't be stupid. And if you phone me again, phone before nine am because I don't like answering the phone later in the day. I only really answer it between seven am and nine am.

Next day I paid the cheque into the bank and you and I went to Sainsbury's. The money lasted months. About a year later – maybe even sooner – she sent me another cheque, this time through the post. I dialled her number and thumbed the ten pence piece into the slot.

Next time only phone me if it's between seven am and nine am, Mrs Shire said.

She sounded quite strict about it.

But Mrs Shire, you'll have to allow me to find a proper way to thank you, I said.

Oh, very proper, she said with a laugh.

In that laugh, I remember, the meaning of the word proper shifted so that properness meant – what? Something witty, something else.

*

Years later, when I'm about to start writing this book, I open The Wrong Music: The Poems of Olive Fraser 1909–77, edited by Helena Mennie Shire, and find, tucked between its front cover and its opening page, two things.

One is an obituary neatly cut out of a newspaper. I don't know now which paper it's from or what its date of publication was, and it's unsigned so I've no idea who wrote it. This is its first paragraph:

Helena Mennie Shire, emeritus fellow of Robinson College, Cambridge University, died on November 16 aged 79. She was born in Aberdeen on June 21, 1912.

That makes it 1991.

The other thing is a postcard, a reproduction of a mosaic of the Healing of the Paralytic of Cafarnao from the Basilica of St Appollinaris New (6th century): that's what it says on the back.

The mosaic is a picture in what looks like two halves but what's really a display of connecting perspectives. On its right hand side two men in tunics are balanced on the edge of the roof of a tall brick building and are hoisting with ropes a bed that's below them. The bed is hanging in mid air with a man in it. They're either raising it up the side of the building as if they're planning to put him on its roof, or they're lowering him off the roof. The man in the bed looks quite calm. He's holding his arms out and open, for balance, or as if to receive something or someone.

On the left hand side, in a mountainous rich green landscape, two finely-dressed men, one with a halo made of little white and green stones, are watching the raising or lowering of the man in the bed and holding their hands up in blessing.

On the back of the card the postmark says 8pm 28 July 1989 and it's addressed in a firm sloped hand to you at your parents' house in Cheam.

Dear Sarah, I was delighted that you did so well in the Tripos. Here's warm good wishes for the next stage LET ME KNOW, PLEASE. I thought you'd appreciate the fine bit of stage-management overleaf. Are you going to do Alison's play about the supermarket girls? Sorry to be so late in writing but I've had a useless right hand for weeks – now back in action. Helena Shire.

Underneath this, it says, like an afterthought,
Tell Alison to write a radioplay on <u>Olive</u>.
Over the years I've tried several times to
interest radio people in such a radio play, as yet
with no luck.

*

Cambridge. Isn't it all spies and homosexuals?
my Aunt Mattie said to my mother when my
mother told her I'd got a postgraduate place.
Cambridge, *the foundation of gold and silver
seemed deep enough; the pavement laid solidly over
the wild grasses* : that's Virginia Woolf, in A Room
of One's Own, not my Aunt Mattie. When I first
went, and one of my friends from Aberdeen
University came to visit me and opened
a hardback copy I'd bought in Heffers,
of TS Eliot's Collected Poems, she gave me
a hard time about my having written my name
in the front with the word *Cambridge* after it.
Cambridge: an affectation and a place.
I hadn't even known what it would look like.

I hadn't even seen pictures. I'd had no ambition to go there rather than anywhere else; I applied because I'd won a scholarship at Aberdeen which meant I'd get a book grant if I went to a Cambridge college called Newnham. The letter that had come for me from the English Faculty telling me I'd been given a place had been signed by someone called Heather Glen. I'd thought it was probably a practical joke.

My father and I drove south in his Mini Metro van one day in October in 1985, late October because I'd been unwell and had missed the first fortnight of term. I don't think the highlands ever looked more beautiful to me than on that cold morning; it was as if I'd never really seen them before. We passed through the Grampians before seven am and we saw the mists furl themselves back off the lochs and the treeless hills in a display of perfect autumn. By the time we got to Cambridge about half past four in the afternoon it was summer, it was 24 degrees, there were people wandering about in shorts and tee-shirts, ten days till November and the leaves still bright green.

The scholarship I'd won was called the Lucy Scholarship; you could only claim it if you went to Newnham (if you were female, Peterhouse if you were male) because its donor, a student at Peterhouse, had met his wife Lucy when she'd been a student at Newnham decades ago. The application form had been full of mysterious questions about colleges and preferences. I'd gone to see the head of the English Faculty in Aberdeen, who knew about Cambridge. Newnham's one of the single sex colleges, he said. A stupid idea, unnecessary, I'd thought with that arrogance we all have when we've done well and we're young and we think we've done it by ourselves and that any history and politics that went before us had nothing to do with it.

I happened to be allocated accommodation in Cambridge with a girl who'd studied science at Newnham as an undergraduate and had stayed on as a postgraduate; we ended up sharing houses all through the years we were graduate students there. I said this to her pretty soon after we met – *single sex colleges, stupid idea* – and she told me very simply what it was like studying science in an environment where most of your teachers were male and most of your classes were heavily gender-imbalanced.

Then she told me what it meant to be taught by someone who was female, then what it meant to be a woman studying metallurgy at all when and where you were the only female postgraduate in the whole department.

Ah, I said.

(She's now Professor of Structural Materials at the University of Southampton.)

And Newnham was where Sylvia Plath had come, in the 1950s, as a Fulbright scholar. When I remembered this I was deeply excited (*she wasn't well liked*, a Newnham porter once told me shaking his head, *it was the sex*). There was a statue in the rose garden which Plath had even written a story about. Stone Boy With

Dolphin. It was a real statue! It was still there!
And I had read that story when I was seventeen
and writing my sixth year studies dissertation on
links between Plath's poetry and her fiction, and
I remembered now how her heroine had gone
out on cold mornings in the story and wiped the
frost from the eyes of the statue. I went out,
myself, one cold morning, to examine what the
frost on the eyes looked like, and felt annoyed
and cheated that even though the whole garden
was frosted over there was no frost on the eyes
of the boy at all.

I was that narrow. I was that literal. I was a
hopeless mix of literal and anti-institutional.
It wouldn't be long before I'd be too
academically undisciplined for Cambridge.
I was studying writers from Ireland and
America – more than one place. I was studying
poetry and fiction – more than one genre.
Soon, as well as being too interdisciplinary for
words, I'd also be being warned repeatedly
about being *too creative*.

The first Christmas I came home to
Inverness my mother surprised me by saying
gently, as she came out of the bathroom one
Saturday night in her bathrobe and was passing
me in the hall, you don't have to do well there
you know, you've already done fine. It won't
matter a bit if you don't.

Either she was psychic or the blackness
round my eyes, my new thinness, my
underconfidence, wasn't as invisible as I'd
banked on. But that she said anything to me at
all is interesting.

The highlands: a great education in what's
not said, in how not to say.

Inverness: capital of the highlands.
Most beautiful place in the world. Place whose
beauty can both heal and hurt the heart.
Succinctly described by Neal Ascherson as a
town suspended between its hospital, its
asylum and its cemetery. The hospital,
Raigmore, I've come to know well over the
years. The asylum, Craig Dunain,

a spread of mid-nineteenth-century architecture across a patchwork of fields and woods, was way up Craig Phadraig up across the canal, right at the centre of the green hilly view from our kitchen window the whole time I grew up. The cemetery, Tomnahurich, is where both my parents are now buried and sits at the end of St Valery, the street we lived in. It happens to be a multi-award-winning cemetery for its own beauty. Tomnahurich, the word, is gaelic for hill of the fairies, and it was a place of folklore before it became a burial ground. Two musicians went there one Saturday midsummer night and were having a drink on the slopes, leaning back in the grasses, and a door opened in the side of a hill and a little man came out. He invited them to a party inside the hill, so in they went and played their fiddles and had a fine time drinking with all the charming shining people, and when the party was over out they came on a cold Sunday morning and walked into the town. But the town was somehow different, and by the time they'd reached the church they knew a hundred years had passed in a night and they were men out of time, and at the door of the church they crumbled into two little piles of dust and their fiddles did too, right down to the strings.

The cemetery is partly bordered by the Caledonian Canal and my father and mother are buried in the Catholic part, under an old tree right up against the boundary next to the canal towpath. When we buried my father two years ago, and had come back after the funeral to the cemetery by ourselves for a final visit before we caught the plane south again, we stood at the flower-heap over the soil and watched the tall white mast of a yacht pass smooth and slow beyond. Then a couple of boys walked past on the path. Though we couldn't see them through the foliage we could hear them. They were singing: if you hate the fucking polis clap your hands. Or possibly: if you hate the fucking Polish, clap your hands.

Aberdeen: just over a hundred miles from Inverness. It's where we went shopping for clothes before Marks and Spencers came to Inverness in the late 1970s or early 1980s. It's the place three of my four siblings went to university (one brother went to Edinburgh); our parents, fiercely intelligent people who had had to leave school and go out to work in their early teens, were passionate about us never missing the chances.

Nairn: sixteen miles from Inverness. It has a fantastic white sand beach. It was the right distance when my mother had a new Mini and was running it in when I was five or six years old; she'd pick me up from school and we'd drive to Nairn for a cup of tea in the bus station café then back to Inverness. And they knew about Nairn in Hollywood because Charlie Chaplin had a house in Nairn. When I was nine the Guarisco boys, who were three or four years younger than me, were American and had come with the oil boom to live in Nairn (our families were friends because my brothers and brother-in-law worked at the rig site) told me they'd seen Charlie Chaplin down a lane near their house. He'd been feeding some ponies over a fence. What did he look like? I said, did he have the black moustache and the funny hat and the shoes, was he walking the funny way? No, they said. He looked like an old man.

Three more moments from my own past which seem somehow pertinent to this story. First: I am upstairs in my father's shop; I'm eleven years old. Downstairs is the shop proper, full of lightbulbs and appliances and batteries. Upstairs is where I get put after school: it's the workshop where all his tools are and where he does small repairs to kettles and toasters on a desk strewn with different sizes of screwdriver, pliers whose noses are reminiscent of reptiles or dinosaurs, bits of rubber-covered wire with their gold strands as fine as hair but sharp and stiff sticking out of the ends where the rubber's been stripped open; and my favourite,

a phial of mercury which I like to open and
pour little spills out of to watch how the shape
the mercury makes forms and reforms when you
poke it with a screwdriver. I can hear him
talking and laughing with a customer down in
the shop; my father's laugh is an open welcome
I'm used to hearing but I can tell he actually
really likes whoever's come in this time. He calls
me downstairs. He's talking and laughing with a
round-faced man in a tweed jacket. Here, Ali, he
says, this man's a writer, he wrote the book
about the hill of the red fox. My dad wires this
man's house. He wires the houses of some other
writers too; a lady poet called Mrs Caird who
lives across the river, and the man who wrote the
book about the otters, Ring of Bright Water, who
lives in the middle of nowhere and is well known
(like the people who talk to their vegetables at
Findhorn) for being *a bit funny*. The man who
wrote the book about the fox shakes my hand.
I thought you'd like to meet him, my father says
to me in the car on the way home.

Next: I'm sitting halfway up a wall in a ruined turret in a small roofless castle, reading a book. I'm twenty-one. Because I have a car, a 2CV, I can go where I like (when the car will actually start) and often I'll drive a carful of friends or sometimes I come alone out here to this ruin north of Aberdeen. Here nobody cares how high you climb up the stony walls, which are full of good footholds, good places to sit and read that aren't the library. We found it one day by chance; we were driving randomly about and we followed a small sign saying Tolquhoun Castle with a silhouette of a turret on it. If the weather's good it's full of suntraps and it's possible to stay here for hours and never see anybody else. I've read most of the books on the syllabus for the Modern Scottish Literature paper here. George Douglas Brown, J MacDougall Hay, Lewis Grassic Gibbon, Neil Gunn, James Kennaway, George Mackay Brown, Robin Jenkins, Gordon Williams, William McIlvanney, Muriel Spark. (Twenty-five years later I'll be on a radio programme where two invited guests each suggest that the other read and comment on a book of their choice. I'll be on with a TV executive who's something to do with Big Brother. I'll choose the great Scottish twentieth century classic Sunset Song by Lewis Grassic Gibbon; he'll choose Joseph Andrews by Henry Fielding. I'll enjoy re-reading and talking about Fielding, a writer I read everything by back in my junior honours year at Aberdeen. But when it comes to talking about Grassic Gibbon, he'll square up to me quite aggressively and say: but it's so Scottish, I felt, the whole time I was reading it, why should I <u>have</u> to read something so very Scottish, I'm just not interested in it, there's nothing in it to interest me. In the end the programme will air with his comments edited out and I will be relieved because I'm ashamed at myself not being quick enough to demolish his argument. In truth I'll sit there with my mouth hanging open too taken aback to do anything but stop myself swearing out loud on Radio 4.)

Next: I'm on a bench in the gardens at
Newnham, I'm twenty-four and I'm having an
argument with my new friend – who is English,
goes to this college too, studies French, Latin and
Dutch, is five years younger than me and still
knows more about books, though I like to pride
myself that I know more about life – about
whether Virginia Woolf is any good or not.
I've never read Woolf before; this first springtime
I've spent in the south I'm reading her for the
first time and I'm much more interested in James
Joyce, so I'm taking her to task about her distaste
at the gutsiness of Bloom while she gently insists
back at me that Woolf's structural genius and
sense of what reality is are just as important, just
as good, and not stolen from Joyce at all. I am
holding forth about class and authenticity,
authority and Englishness, I am waving Mrs
Dalloway in the air. I feel I'm in the right; at
Aberdeen Woolf was, I sensed from the majority
of my teachers, rather frowned on as a bit
dilletante at best. I won't realise my own

prejudice till four or five years later when I'm teaching a university class in Glasgow about Woolf's novels and I hear and recognise, in much of the class's determined inverted snobbery, the same lines I said then. But for now I'm holding cleverly-stupidly forth to this girl, the Englishness of whose voice is strangely attractive to me, in this garden where I can't stop thinking uneasily about the word privilege, in this town with its market square full of fruits I'd never actually tasted before coming here, cherries, greengages, and its landscape that radiates out and away from it with skies huger and bluer and calmer than I've known, not a mountain in sight, and I'm surprised at myself secretly, in spite of where I'm from, for really actually quite liking it here, not that I'd ever say so to anybody.

*

Helena Shire was a Scot, whose life was devoted to the literature and music of her land. She knew and loved literature from the medieval and renaissance

periods in the Scots tongue. Through her publication
of texts from manuscripts or inaccessible old print
she brought to a wider public the glories of the
renaissance flowering of culture in Scotland.

The paragraphs in this section in italics are
from the obituary I found with the postcard in
Olive Fraser's book.

She grew up in Aberdeen and graduated from the
university there in 1933 as a gold medallist. From
Aberdeen she went to Cambridge University to take
up a scholarship at Newnham College where she
gained a first class in the English Tripos and started
her career in research.

In a memoir published in a festscrift for
Helena Shire's 79th birthday, her brother
comments on how, because she was born on
midsummer day, her parents named her after
Helena in A Midsummer Night's Dream.
He recalls growing up in a house whose loud
communal polyphony was a mix of Shakespeare
and Burns and WS Gilbert and Scottish folk
song and psalms and the general clatter of every

family meal. He remembers a story about his sister mixing, by mistake, a precious wartime sack of oatmeal with a big bottle of perfume (by jumping on the sack, which looked like it'd be really good to jump on, and not seeing the perfume, a gift, balanced there on top). She was in big trouble for that. But the oatcakes the perfumed oatmeal went into making were, he said, like oatcakes never tasted before and never tasted again.

At Aberdeen University she served for two years on the student council representing women students in Arts. She was a creative writer herself, winning the University short story prize two years in a row. Her story, Corbeau, published in the student magazine, Alma Mater, in 1930, is a sharp little morality tale about education, kindness, religion, survival, above all about getting your priorities right.

She arrived in Cambridge a decade and a half before women were permitted full degrees and university membership (which was how things were for the first seven and a quarter centuries of its existence as a university, from 1209 to 1947). Her dissertation at Newnham, her first sustained research work, was on the Bedlam Ballads, and was entitled Garland for Tom o' Bedlam.

She told us, once, about her coming to Newnham and about how the girls in the '30s, not being allowed to do their own laundry, had to trunk it up regularly and send it off to be done at home. So you needed a lot of clothes, she said, just to see you through the weeks. She told us, too, about a visit Virginia Woolf made to Newnham in the years she was a student there. The rumour went round that Woolf was coming to take tea in the room of one of the girls and a lot of jostling went on for invites. A small crowd of girls gathered excitedly in the room. They waited and they waited. At last Woolf arrived, she swept into the room, she swept past the girls as if they weren't there, swept up to a window and she sat at it gazing out of it with her chin in her hand as if there was no one else in the room. Someone poured tea and handed her a cup. She took it and turned back to the window. Then, after a time and without saying a single word to anyone, she drank her tea, stood up and swept straight out of the room again.

How we read things. I've always loved this vision of Woolf's recalcitrance. First I took it as proof of her snobby exclusivity. Later in life I took it as proof of her unruffleable mercuriality, her rightful impatience with and intractability at others' demands on her. And then, this summer, while I was reading A Room of One's Own again, her book about women and education, specifically often about Newnham itself and written in the years just before Helena Shire came to Newnham, I read, with new eyes, this – in which Woolf is trying to imagine the tactics necessary for free observation which her imaginary female proto-novelist, Mary Carmichael, might need to call on when it came to depicting her own gender:

For I wanted to see how Mary Carmichael set to work to catch those unrecorded gestures, those unsaid or half-said words which form themselves, no more palpably than the shadows of moths on the ceiling, when women are alone, unlit by the capricious and coloured light of the other sex. She will need to hold her breath, I said, reading on, if she is to do it; for women are so suspicious of any interest that has not some obvious motive behind it, so terribly accustomed to concealment and suppression, that they are off at the flicker of an eye turned observingly in their direction. The only way for you to do it, I thought, addressing Mary Carmichael as if she were there, would be to talk of something else, looking steadily out of the window, and thus note, not with a pencil in a notebook, but in the shortest of shorthand, in words that are

hardly syllabled yet, what happens when
Olivia – this organism that has been
under the shadow of the rock these
million years – feels the light fall on it,
and sees coming her way a piece of
strange food – knowledge, adventure, art.

Woolf says this in a book about how *intellectual
freedom depends upon material thing*s, about the
cost of education; the losses, over generations
for the artist or scholar who happened,
in history, to be a woman; the possibility for
change; and above all about the importance of
legacy – very practical legacy – since A Room
of One's Own is as much about legacy as it's
about politics, as much about cash in hand as
it's about words on the page.

   Not long after A Room of One's Own
was being written and published, Helena
Mennie got married, became Mrs Shire,
had children and continued teaching at a
time when this combination was still

practically impossible, near unheard-of.

For the rest of her life she lived in Cambridge, where she researched, wrote, lectured and taught in the English faculty. From 1961 to 1963 she was a senior fellow in arts of the Carnegie Trust for the universities of Scotland. She always taught part time, keeping most of her working time for research.

Even as late as in 1978 when she published her seminal casebook about Edmund Spenser's poetry, A Preface to Spenser, and she'd been teaching for four decades, was now an internationally renowned expert in European medieval and renaissance literatures, she still chose to describe herself in the biographical paragraph at the front of this book as a student.

The partnership of music and words was important to her as may be seen in her editing of the song texts for <u>Music of Scotland 1500-1700, Musica Britannica Vol XV.</u> During that period, Scotland was ruled by the Stuart monarchs, at whose courts, especially during the sixteenth century, poetry and music flourished. Her book,

now recognised as a classic authority, <u>Song, Dance</u>
<u>and Poetry of the Court of Scotland under King</u>
<u>James VI</u>, reveals how well she understood the arts
in sixteenth century Scotland, and their relationship
with the arts of France, England and Italy.
This power to see literature within the wider context
appears also in her <u>Preface to Spenser</u> in which
she gives due recognition to the Irish influence in
the life and work of the English poet.

Her work on Spenser focuses not just on
his understanding of and respect for the
misunderstood culture of an Ireland he came
to love, but also on the loss of allusive
understanding and the possible re-florescence
of it, over time, between readerships. She draws
attention to a complex layering of number
systems in his poetry, in theme and form both.
She comments, here, on patronage of the arts:
for patronage, she writes on page 33, considering
Spenser's pride, his impecuniary demise, his
exhausted and impoverished death in 1599,
is support of a creative writer so that he may write

his poetry, 'grace coming and grace returned'.

But the real heart of A Preface to Spenser lies in the simple act of restoration, a making available of the allusive layered quality of Spenser's work to a naïve modern reader, since *the reader who has sampled James Joyce's Ulysses will find he is on known ground,* she says, suggesting that lovers of Joyce, Kafka and Orwell will all feel at home with Spenser.

This is how you remember being taught by her in the late 1980s when I ask you to write about it for this piece:

> I remember going to Mrs Shire's room in college. It was on a walkway in a part of college that I wasn't used to. It felt more surrounded by brick than other parts of the college. More like a medieval castle. She taught the boys separately from the girls and so I remember how we (the girls) sat in this room and she talked about the middle English texts we were to study and asked us

questions about what we knew about the Bible and Greek myths, what references we could see in the texts. She revealed to us that we couldn't study literature without first knowing the Bible and mythology and I remember leaving the lesson feeling chastened and that I should read a Bible straightaway, a Bible that contained ALL the books of the Bible – I had been given for the first time the idea that I should be rigorous. To me then Mrs Shire felt like she knew everything but she wasn't going to give it away easily. I remember her then like I remember my first visit to the university library – something monolithic that I had no idea how to use.

I've been reading Mrs Shire's books about Spenser and the Scottish renaissance court all summer, been far out at sea in a time and a subject I know next to nothing about. But it's clear even to me that her work on the nearly-lost

Scottish court tradition of music and poetry, a tradition blasted away to almost nothing by years of Reformation, makes Shire's academic work properly pioneering. She wrote extensively about the forgotten traditions of part-music (music for more than one voice) and art-music (as opposed to simply religious music) and she found and published enough unpublished works not just to form an alternative tradition, one that nobody believed existed, and not just to trace, as she put it, *in bright threads,* clear connections between this tradition and the other European courtly traditions from north to south, but to establish this tradition in, of all places, Cambridge – a place not exactly used to accepting alternative traditions.

Many of Helena Shire's discoveries were of small manuscripts or single poems and some of these she published in the series The Ninth of May. These editions are now sought after by bibliophiles.

The Ninth of May pamphlets are a series of short works published between the sixties and

the seventies by Sebastian Carter at the
Rampant Lions Press. Carter had been a
student of Shire's; she encouraged him to take
up printing on his father's press. The series'
title comes from a celebration of integrating
cultures, from a line of poetry by Dunbar, from
The Thrissill and the Rois, a work written to
welcome a summer marriage of northern and
southern cultures, of James IV of Scotland and
Princess Margaret Tudor, the sister of Henry
VIII. *Off lusty May upon the nynt morrow.*
They're beautiful artefacts, the pamphlets, as
well as important sources for reassemblage of
scattered pieces of otherwise unrecorded works;
they consist of finds like the fragment of song
written *on a leaf from an Account Book of a Tailor
and Draper for the years 1535-36, used in binding
the oldest Record Book of the Corporation of
Tenterden in Kent.* (Some pieces were collected
and published for the first time *from the
manuscripts of Alexander Forbes of Tolquhon,*
in whose ruined grand house I'd sat so often

without a clue where I was, in my Aberdeen
years, reading Scottish writing of a different
time in its sheltered sunspots.)

*The war gave Helena Shire the task of teaching
English to exiled Polish men and women who
wanted to join the British armed forces. Her
friendship with them continued to the end of her life.
She helped bring to fruition the Corbridge Trust,
named after her husband, which fosters exchanges
between British and Polish universities. She was
awarded Silver Insignia of the Order of Merit of the
Republic of Poland.*

I remember her saying how exciting it was
to teach the servicemen and women in the war,
people who'd otherwise never have seen
university, never mind Cambridge.

I remember you and I going to her house one
afternoon and her showing us a photograph in a
frame, of herself and her sister, young girls, out
on a hill with another older girl, a woman, all in
walking gear. That's Nan Shepherd, she said.
I nearly choked on my tea; I'd just been reading

Shepherd, a great Scottish writer of the '20s
and '30s who'd been completely out of print
for decades and was only just coming back
into print fifty years later, like Willa Muir,
whom I mentioned. Oh, Willa, she said, yes.
Really? I said. You knew Willa Muir too?
And Edwin Muir?

Next to the photo of the girls on the hill with
Nan Shepherd there was one of Mrs Shire,
but her older self, herself now, holding her sides
and hooting with laughter in black and white.

During the last ten years of her life Helena Shire
turned to Scottish poetry of the twentieth century.
She edited two selections, The Pure Account and
The Wrong Music, from the fine poetry written by
Olive Fraser who had also achieved high honours
at the universities of Aberdeen and Cambridge.
This work was done from affection for her former
classmate, yet Helena Shire's scholarly searching
eye and critical faculty were as clear as ever.

One day in the 1930s Helena Mennie was
crossing the street in Cambridge and she saw

her friend Olive Fraser standing in the doorway
of a department store. But she was strange.
She was dressed as a shepherdess, but in her
old Harris tweed as well. She was carrying a
long shepherd's crook and had her hair done
up like a Viking warrior. On her feet she was
wearing delicate silver dancing-sandals.

*She was closely associated with Robinson
College from its beginnings in the early 1970s
and became one of its first fellows on its formal
creation in 1977. Her college life was many
faceted: she taught English, selected the books
for the English section of the library, took an
active interest in the gardens and fabric of the
college, designed the college crest and endowed
a photographic competition.*

One student turned up one day offering her
a brace of pheasants instead of an essay.
I don't know if she accepted; I'd like to know.
The poet Thom Gunn remembers her kindly
in his autobiographical writing about his time
at university, where he *read the whole of*

Shakespeare, and doing that, Helena Shire later remarked, adds a cubit to anybody's stature.
Gunn, in turn, wrote a poem dedicated to her.
It's about the pagan act of churchbuilding,
a reconciliation of opposing forces, the spirit
of otherness, the itch and seminality of
something other at the core of any tradition
or institution. He called it The Antagonism.

*

I'm not going to quote the last paragraph of the
obituary, the end of things with its predeceasings
and its deceasing. Instead, here are some of her
favourite words, words that turn up again and
again in her writing.

Precarious is one. Affinities is another. And
currency is a word that crops up a lot and a
word she uses on an inventive scale. She uses
it to mean money and worth; she uses it to
mean time. She uses it to mean a flow of
energy. Rediscovered works, released from
obscurity back into circulation, are a currency.

The relationship between words and music over time is a long and lively currency. Songs travel, changing their form, becoming new songs, by vocal currency.

I went onto Abe Books before I began work on this book, and found the Ninth of May pamphlets and bought them all. They'd survived the decades perfectly. They cost me a fair whack of currency.

I had these beautiful pamphlets for only a month. Then one day in summer I came into my study after a couple of weeks away and I realised I maybe shouldn't have left them in the sunlight at the window. The sun had faded all the bits of the covers of the pamphlets it could reach: precarious.

A shire, Chambers c20th Dictionary tells me, is an administrative district of England formed for mainly taxation purposes by the Anglo-Saxons, or a county, or a rural district having its own elected council, from the Old English word scir, meaning office or authority. It's a suffix, and allied to the words shear, shore and share.

Inverness-shire, Nairnshire, Aberdeenshire, Cambridgeshire, and all the shires traversed between them from north to south and north again. We met only five times in all and she treated me like family. That's kindness, a word in which family and generosity meet as affinities.

I sense she'd be annoyed at me having written so much about her here. So I'll sidestep into another's voice and quote Woolf one last time.

Who shall measure the heat and violence of the poet's heart when caught and tangled in a woman's body?

When I was a small child I looked out of our kitchen window and I saw every day without seeing, without knowing – I know now – the place where Helena Shire's friend, the poet, happened to be at a time in her life.

When I was a young woman and at a bit of a loss in a new country, an older woman I didn't know and who didn't know me gave me this

open commission. She paid me handsomely
for it at the time.

Grace coming, grace returned.

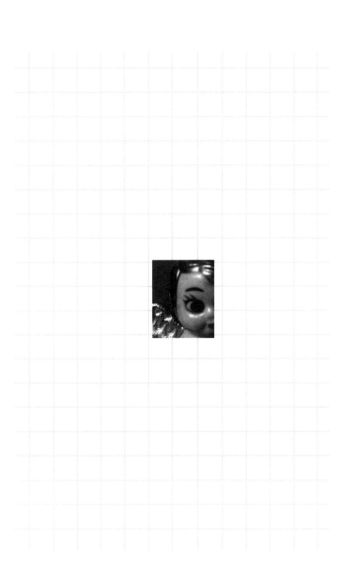

The wound

Once there was a man in a poem written in
the late 1500s by Alexander Montgomerie, a
poet who at one point in his life taught the
young King James the Ist of England and the
VIth of Scotland how to write mellifluous
musical sonnets and how to craft all sorts of
poetic forms.

This man was in a landscape full of a
birdsong so mirthful and melodious that that's
what made him stay there lying back in the
grass, just hearing them sing, watching them
wing themselves above him so high in the
beautiful sky.

The place was full of other creatures too,
a hare nibbling at the flowers, cats, foxes, deer,
some creatures whose names are Scots words
or usages that I've never heard (a cunning?

a fowmart?); in any case all the creatures in the place went about their business – eating what they needed and fearing other creatures who might hurt them and skowping all fra brae to brae – in pairs, and the air was so warm, the flowers so flourishing, all bloom-opened and coloured-up for May, all in a stanza structure whose repeated pattern is such a counterpointing of internal rhyme and syllabic falling-away that it's not surprising that a metamorphic allusion to the story of Narcissus and Echo, the one forever emptily lamenting, the other pining to death at the unhaveability of his own reflected face, comes surfacing in a poem about such a paradise as soon as stanza number four.

Never mind tragedies like those, though. Look at the dew, so twinklingly like diamonds on every twirl of foliage; look at the flowers falling over themselves to bloom so that the bees, clever creatures, could keep themselves well-fed now and ready for winter too with their precise, wise storing of the pollen in their hives.

It was a place of such beauty and pleasure that it was probably a sight only poets would be able to describe, and I'm no poet, me, the man in the poem says, modest. And on top of all this there was a river too, in the form of a remarkable waterfall shooting out of a craggy cliff of rock and tumbling and rumbling down into a deep crevasse; and the sound of that water was also a kind of music, but one that had a harmony no musician could ever match, a set of descants not even the legendary fountain of the Muses at Helicon could rival.

That's what all those birds were shouting about in their birdsong. In fact, some of those songlarks were holding forth so loudly about it, flying so very high in the sky, that they woke Cupid, who'd been asleep and who sat up, got up, stretched and descended, came down to earth there and then and stood in front of the man in the poem.

He was gentle. He was childlike. He was so

small his bow was only a three-quarter one, not full-size. He looked like a saint, with his quiver hanging by his bare thigh and his two pretty gold wings growing between his shoulders. He shook the bow-brace off his left arm, dropped his quiver and arrows and bow, took off his wings and laid everything out in the grass and the meadow-flowers. The man felt himself suddenly huge and stout beside this small perfect being. He gawked at the stuff on the ground. Cupid laughed; he didn't even have to try, did he? The man was bought and sold already.

I'm Cupid, he said smiling (like there was anybody in the world who didn't know exactly who he was). So, what would you like? The wings? The arrows? Some fire-tips? Very effective at setting things alight.

Oh, I'd never be able to afford any of this, the man said.

For nothing, Cupid said. Free, to you. But I'll need it all back when you're done, if that's okay.

The god picked up the wings first because he'd seen how the man couldn't take his eyes off them. He bound them hard on to the man's back. He held out the arrows in the quiver and the tips of them were lit and shining like a dozen tiny torches. He slapped the man on the back, between the wings.

Break a leg, he said.

Up the man went with the bow in his hands, like Icarus on the wing, up and up he went. As he soared above the tops of trees, the cliff, the clouds, he drew an arrow. He strung it, stretched it and aimed it.

But god knows what happened, because the next thing he did was somehow shoot himself in the chest by mistake.

Ouch.

He hovered in mid-air. He touched the wound with his hand. It was small, but it really hurt. He touched it again. No, it really did hurt to do that. He told himself not to do it again, then he did it again. Ouch.

Every time he touched the wound it burnt
him more, and he couldn't stop. A moth,
he thought, and a flame, that's what I am,
I'm both moth and flame at once, and down
he went blunt and hurt, singed and dwindling
through the air like a stone, like the wingless
breast of a bird.

He landed so hard on the ground that up
went the dust and off went the creatures
running away in all directions. When the dust
cleared Cupid was standing there laughing,
his hands on his hips.

Welcome home! he said.

The man lay shivering on the ground.
Cupid picked his things up, tore the perfect
wings off, threw them over his own bare
shoulder where they settled and folded
themselves like happy golden doves on his back.

The man on the ground heard the god's
laughter fade, watched the god fly higher and
higher till he couldn't be seen any more.
The pain in his chest turned to langour turned

to torment turned to sadness turned to
madness turned to anger, to despair.

It was the end.

Of course, it wasn't the end at all. It was only
page 11 of 54, it was only stanza fourteen of one
hundred and eleven, it was truly very early on in
the story, in which the man will soon face a
choice between climbing for a beautiful bunch of
cherries on a tree, so high up on the rocks above
the waterfall that they're nigh unreachable, and
reaching out to pick a bitter black bunch of sloes
on a bush, very easily available at the foot of the
cherry tree. Before he'll choose, though, there'll
be a long discourse between a whole villageworth
of quite longwinded personifications whose
names are Hope, Despair, Dread, Danger,
Courage, Wisdom, Melancholy, Reason, Wit,
Experience and Will, and who'll all hang about
round the fevered man, holding forth about
which they think he should choose and why.
Then at the very end, when he's made the choice
between whether he'll go for the dangerous

cherries or accept the easy option, those cherries, which have ripened by themselves in the meantime, will fall off the tree and straight into his hands.

But for now he was alone and hurt and broken on the ground, the man, gravely wounded. Worse, he knew himself a fool, knew himself a loser, knew himself too late, and defeated, ruined by his own hand, near to death.

It was the end and then this happened. The wound in his chest, red and burning, open like an eye, an ear, a mouth, began to glow.

It glowed and warmed until it embered him. Flowers closest to where he lay started to wilt in the heat of it. But inside the man, the heat changed into something else. The first thing he felt it become was courage and the next thing was desire.

They went through him, but with a roughness he'd never known. Then instead of in pain he was thirsty, but with a thirst he'd never known. The heat and the glow and the thirst combined and melted the man into someone he'd never been.

He heard a noise. It was the roar of water.

Up he got off the ground to go and sort himself out.

Some of the books used as sources for this book:

Jane Chance (ed.) *Women Medievalists and the Academy,* Wisconsin 2005

James Cranstoun (ed.) *The Poems of Alexander Montgomerie,* Edinburgh 1887

Kenneth Elliott and Helena Mennie Shire (eds.) *Musica Britannica: A National Collection of Music, XV: Music of Scotland 1500-1700,* London 1957

Alisoun Gardner-Medwin and Janet Hadley Williams (eds.) *A Day Estivall : essays on the Music, Poetry and History of Scotland and England and Poems previously unpublished, in honour of Helena Mennie Shire,* Aberdeen 1990

Thom Gunn, *The Occasions of Poetry: Essays in Criticism and Autobiography,* London 1982

F R Hart and J B Pick, *Neil M. Gunn :A Highland Life,* London 1981

Ann Phillips (ed.) *A Newnham Anthology,* Cambridge 1979

Walter Scott, *The Heart of Mid-Lothian,* Edinburgh 1871 *Ivanhoe, A Romance,* Edinburgh 1871

Helena Mennie Shire, *Song, Dance & Poetry of the Court of Scotland Under King James VI,* Cambridge 1969; *A Preface to Spenser,* London and New York 1978; (ed.) *Poems From Panmure House,* Ninth of May, Cambridge 1960; (ed.) *Poems and Songs of Sir Robert Ayton,* Ninth of May, Cambridge 1961 (ed.) *The Thrissil, the Rois and the Flour-de- lys,* Ninth of May, Cambridge 1962 (ed.) *King Orphius and Sir Colling,* Ninth of May, Cambridge 1973 (ed.) *The Pure Account: Poems of Olive Fraser,* Aberdeen University Press 1981 (ed.) *The Wrong Music: The Poems of Olive Fraser 1909 – 77,* Canongate 1989

J C Smith and E De Selincourt (eds.) *The Poetical Works of Edmund Spenser,* Oxford 1912

Virginia Woolf, *A Room of One's Own,* London, 1929

125

First published in 2013 by Full Circle Editions
Design and Layout © Full Circle Editions 2013
Parham House Barn, Brick Lane, Framlingham, Woodbridge,
Suffolk IP13 9LQ
www.fullcircle–editions.co.uk
"The beholder" was originally commissioned by the Durham Literary
Festival and is published here with acknowledgement and thanks.

A CIP record for this book is available from the British Library.

Set in Plantin Light & Gill Sans
Paper: Olin rough 120gsm FSC® Mix Credit

Book design: Jonathan Christie

Printed and bound in Suffolk by Healeys Print Group, Ipswich

ISBN 978-0-9571528-2-3

Note on the typeface:
Plantin Light is part of the Monotype Plantin family, a modern revival
typeface that was first cut in 1913. Its origins date back to the 16th
century, specifically to serif typefaces cut by Robert Granjon, and is
named after Christophe Plantin (1520—1589), an influential
Renaissance humanist, book printer and publisher. It is one of the
typefaces that influenced the creation of Times Roman and today
features a full suite of small caps, ligatures and old style figures.